CONCORD PUBLIC LIBRARY
45 GREEN STREET
CONCORD, NH 03301

To Hayden and Hyatt,
Have fun discovering the talents God has given you!
Love, Uncle Cuy

"But each man has his own gift from God;
one has this gift, another has that."

1 CORINTHIANS 7:7

ZONDERKIDZ

The Goat of Many Colors
Copyright © 2010 by Cuyler Black

Requests for information should be addressed to:
Zonderkidz, *Grand Rapids, Michigan 49530*

Library of Congress Cataloging-in-Publication Data

Black, Cuyler.
    The goat of many colors / by Cuyler Black.
        p.   cm.
    Summary: A flamingo, continually interrupted by an anteater, tells a story of
a talented goat who, through a misunderstanding, becomes leader of a herd of
wild goats and realizes that his talent is a gift from God.
    ISBN 978-0-310-71634-1 (hardcover : alk. paper)
    [1. Ability—Fiction. 2. Animals—Fiction. 3. Christian life—Fiction. 4. Humorous
stories.] I. Title.
PZ7.B556Goc 2010
[E]—dc22   2008048895

All Scripture quotations, unless otherwise indicated, are taken from the Holy Bible,
New International Version®, NIV®. Copyright © 1973, 1978, 1984 by Biblica, Inc.™
Used by permission of Zondervan. All rights reserved worldwide.

Any Internet addresses (websites, blogs, etc.) and telephone numbers printed in
this book are offered as a resource. They are not intended in any way to be or imply
an endorsement by Zondervan, nor does Zondervan vouch for the content of these
sites and numbers for the life of this book.

All rights reserved. No part of this publication may be reproduced, stored in a re-
trieval system, or transmitted in any form or by any means—electronic, mechanical,
photocopy, recording, or any other—except for brief quotations in printed reviews,
without the prior permission of the publisher.

Zonderkidz is a trademark of Zondervan.

Editor: Mary Hassinger
Art direction and design: Kris Nelson

Printed in China

10 11 12 13 14 15 /GPC/ 10 9 8 7 6 5 4 3 2 1

The Goat of Many Colors

Written & Illustrated by Cuyler Black

He means "COAT of Many Colors." It's a story in the Bible about a boy named Joseph.

Well, it's not quite that story. Shush! Let's get started.

ZONDERkidz

ZONDERVAN.com/
AUTHORTRACKER
follow your favorite authors

Meanwhile, Jacob the landowner decided to give a special gift to his favorite son, Joseph.

Jacob owned a beautiful coat.

Gus didn't know what was happening. Shocked and frightened, he escaped from the servant and ran away.
Gus kept running and running far into the desert, until he realized he was very lost.
He must be thirsty. He should have packed some ant juice.

Gus enjoyed being the top goat. Whatever he wanted, he got. Whatever he told them to do, they did. It was very good to be king of the goats.

The goats learned that God had given each of them talents. Maybe they couldn't all dive like Gus, but some could sing, and some could dance. Some could draw, and some were really good at math. They only needed to discover their talents and share them!

2+2 =4

My talent is telling jokes-- original jokes!

You have a talent for interrupting, that's what you have.

Hey, what happened to the old servant who was supposed to fetch the coat of many colors?

Oh, he realized that he made a mistake hearing "goat."

 So he brought Jacob the coat?

Not exactly.

Other funny stuff from Cuyler Black

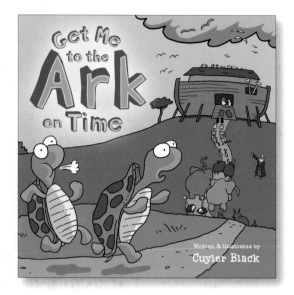

PJ PBC

FEB 18 2011

APR 29 2011

PENACOOK

Get Me to the Ark on Time
978-0310-71633-4

Laugh along with the narrators Anteater and Flamingo as they tell this exciting tale of Noah and the Ark from a slightly different perspective.

What's that Funny Look on Your Faith?
978-0310-81397-2

A Far Side-type comic romp through the Bible. Young and old will find it laugh-out-loud funny and a great way to present faith to those who think believers need to "lighten up!"

Send-A-Laugh Postcards

- Church Life Cartoon Postcards, 978-0310-82275-2
- Special Occasion Cartoon Postcards, 978-0310-82407-7
- Old Testament Cartoon Postcards, 978-0310-82408-4
- New Testament Cartoon Postcards, 978-0310-82409-1

Each pack includes 30 postcards that can be torn out and mailed. All 120 original cartoons stand alone as a lighter, humorous look at faith while keeping a respectful tone.

See more Cuyler Black creations at Inheritthemirth.com